I0537548

TIME TRAVEL TRIO

Three Short Stories
by
Sam Knight

Copyright 2013 Sam Knight

Print Edition 2013
Knight Writing Press
KnightWritingPress@gmail.com

ISBN 978-1-62869-009-5

GHOSTS OF TIME© Copyright 2013

JUST IN TIME FOR A CELEBRATION© Copyright 2013

ON THE HEELS OF SPRING HEELED JACK© Copyright 2013

Cover Art© Copyright 2017 Sam Knight

Cover and Interior Design by Knight Writing Press

Interior Art© Copyright 2013 Sam Knight

Spring Heeled Jack images are believed to be in the Public Domain and no infringement is intended.

Author Bio Photo by Stacey Vowell

All rights reserved. No part of this publication may be reproduced or transmitted in any form, electronic, mechanical, or otherwise, including photocopying, recording, or by any information storage and retrieval system, without the express written permission of the copyright holder, with the exception of brief quotations within critical articles and reviews.

This is a work of fiction. Any similarities to real persons, places, or events are coincidental or used fictitiously without intent of any implication.

First Publication June 2013

Published by

Knight Writing Press, an imprint of

Knight Writing LLC

Parker, CO 80134

knightwritingpress@gmail.com

Dedication

For my friends, who continue to help me, and more importantly, encourage me, when I need it the most.

Quincy J. Allen (http://www.quincyallen.com/)

Kevin J. Anderson and Rebecca Moesta (http://www.wordfire.com/)

David Boop (http://www.davidboop.com/)

J. A. Campbell (http://writerjacampbell.wordpress.com/)

Guy Anthony DeMarco (http://guyanthonydemarco.com/)

Pamela M. Nihiser (http://www.facebook.com/pamela.m.nihiser)

Kathryn Renta (http://www.kathrynrenta.com/)

Christopher M. Salas (https://www.facebook.com/CursesAndDemons)

For Peter J. Wacks (http://peterjwacks.com/), whose love of time travel
inspired me.

For Mark Leslie (http://markleslie.ca/), and Kobo for pushing me on to do it myself.

For my critique group, be they No Name Heros, or be they part of the Cariboucrew, who will be sad to see I did not take all of their suggestions to heart.

For my Tribe, who can be found at http://www.authorfriends.com. If you are looking for a new author to try out, I know of no better place to start.

TIME TRAVEL TRIO

Ghosts of Time

17AUG52 08:47

"She was right. It looks like someone finger-painted with spaghetti down here." Roy absently scratched at a long scar across his unshaven chin as he considered the mess. The dead end of the maintenance corridor was covered from the ceiling down with a fine brownish-red spray. Rivulets of red had formed spiderweb patterns on the smooth white surfaces, running down the walls and leaving half dried puddles on the floor.

"It was definitely human." Emily, Roy's second in command, pointed towards the corner where some recognizable pieces had piled up. She tucked a stray curl of her black hair back into her ponytail as she tried to hide her disgust.

Emily and Roy wore identical standard issue athletic pants and shirts. They had been in the middle of their morning sparring session when the emergency alarm sounded, bringing them down to the lowest level of Luna Base.

"What do you suppose happened?" Emily asked.

Roy shook his head. "We've seen some strange shit since we left Earth, and it's only gotten stranger here on Luna. I can't even guess anymore. It's a damn shame to come through everything you have to do to get here—only to end up like that."

"Oh my god." Butkus came up behind them and covered his nose and mouth with the white sleeve of his uniform.

3

"Kinda makes you wish we could open a window." Emily wore a grimace as she glanced back to the Chief Medical Officer.

"At least that would flash freeze it and get rid of the smell," Roy agreed. He wondered if his face had gone as white as both of theirs. The only reason he could bear the shocking sight was that it was nearly unrecognizable.

Butkus, staring at the mess and trying to take it in, shook his head. "Sun's up now. It would boil off." He lost his battle to control his visceral reaction and dropped his portable lab case to the tiled floor with a metallic clatter. Roy and Emily watched as he hurried back out of the small service hallway, retreating towards fresher air and nearly knocking down one of the two men stationed to preserve the scene.

Roy turned back to Emily. "I reckon we need to put eyes on each and every Loonie, find out who this is."

Emily nodded and they both stood silently, grappling with the reality of the mess around them.

"I'm back." Butkus' voice was hoarse. "Sorry. It just hit me hard."

"Any idea what could cause this?" Emily asked Butkus.

Butkus couldn't keep the look of disgust off his face as he shook his head. "The pieces over there indicate a blast force, something that would push them into the corner," he looked around the dead end, "but I don't see any evidence of an explosion. See the vent grill?" He pointed at a plastic cover on the wall. "They made those so light I can poke a finger through them. If a blast capable of doing this," he waved his hand at the red mess, "went off in here, I would expect the grill to be shattered.

"Judging from the amount of … moisture, I'd guess this happened less than twenty-four hours ago." He toed at a dried smear. "It's been here at least five or six hours." Something caught his eye. "Look over there," he pointed behind where Roy and Emily stood. "See the smudge? And the 'reverse shadow' where no drops landed? Someone else was here."

He pulled a DNA sequencer out of his portable med kit. "I'll know who it was that died in about half an hour. It'll take longer to see if I can find any trace of who the other person was."

Roy gave him a dour smile. "Emily and I are going to go do a visual head count. The computer says everyone checked in during the alarm, so I reckon we need to actually put eyes on everyone, just to make sure." Roy turned and left. Emily followed.

4

As soon as they were out of earshot, Emily whispered, "Are you thinking what I'm thinking?"

"That the only way everyone can check in, if one of us is dead, is that someone was monkeying around with the time machine?"

"Got it in one." Emily shook her head as she thought. "I can't even think of who it could have been, or why they would have been down here," Emily mumbled. "The weekly inspection of the conduits found the mess, and there is nothing else down here."

"You don't think someone could have been meeting for a Stim deal or something down here, do you?" Roy asked, but he already knew the answer. Ever since the Information War, individual privacy was closely guarded and zealously protected. Privy booths were available to anyone at any time and Luna base had been designed to make sure people had enough space and privacy they wouldn't go insane during their five year stints. There was no need to seek out a place like this. Assigned quarters would have worked just fine.

"All I can think of is someone attempted sabotage and it blew up in their face. Or it was murder. A very angry murder. Unless you know about some secret project I don't." Emily glanced sideways at Roy.

"More secret than the time machine?" Roy shook his head. As second in command, Emily had been filled in on everything in case something happened to Roy. Hell, even if there was one she didn't know about, he would have told her just to relieve the boredom of being trapped on the friggin' moon.

Emily nodded in understanding. There wasn't anything more secret. Only the two of them, of all the people on the base, knew about it, and it was doubtful more than a hundred people on Earth were privy to the information either. Their conversations had occasionally wandered into areas exploring the idea that they might both be terminated after this mission to protect the secret of the time machine.

Roy echoed her confusion in his own silent thoughts. There were only two hundred Loonies up here on the moon, all one year into their five together, and they were damn near one giant family. What was there to gain by this? Sabotaging the base would kill them all. The Loonies all had specific jobs with no place for promotion up here, there was no money, legal recreational drugs were already supplied. There was little motive for murder Roy could imagine.

"There you are!" Gordon came around the corner ahead of them, shuffling his feet in an awkward penguin walk that always irritated Roy.

"Look at this! Look at these readings!" The head of the research department held up his Portable Data Device for Roy and Emily to see. Emily tried not to roll her eyes and Roy took pity on her, sending her ahead as Gordon pointed to gibberish on his PDD.

"This interference is unexplainable! And look at this spike at three o'clock this morning! It's incredible! We've never even imagined anything like this!"

"Gordon, you know I don't get this stuff. I'm not a scientist, and definitely not a ghost hunter. I don't believe in your ghosts no matter what your machines say, and I have no idea what a spike in your 'ecto-meter' means. So, I need you to take a deep breath, and then, slowly, explain to me why I need to deal with this right now instead of the dead …" Roy started to say body, but there really wasn't one, "person back there."

"Somebody died? That's what the alarm was?" Gordon's eyes lit up and he turned his attention back to his PDD, scrolling through data. "That has to be it! Do we know the exact time of death?"

Roy waited a few more seconds while the scientist was absorbed with the little screen. "I need to go, Gordon. I have a situation to deal with. When you figure out what it was you wanted to tell me, let me know."

Roy stalked off after Emily, leaving Gordon entranced by his PDD.

17AUG52 09:36

"Everyone is accounted for," Emily reported as she entered Roy's office. "I personally have gone around and laid eyes on each and every Loonie just to make damn sure. You're the last person I needed to see for myself. Just to make sure …" She grinned.

Roy looked up from his desk. Emily was still in her gym clothes, not having taken the time to change. Seeing her in them reminded Roy he hadn't changed yet either.

"There's no evidence anyone used the time machine," Roy informed her, "but that don't mean shit. I wish it kept a log. Damn stupid if you ask me."

"Well," Emily dropped into the chair across from Roy and wiped the curl of hair back out of her eye again, "since only the two of us know about it …"

6

"The smear down there has to be one of us." Roy finished the thought for her. He sighed and stared at the simulated window on his sterile white wall. Today it showed a green pasture with cattle in front of the Rocky Mountains. The image did nothing to relax him. It was completely devoid of warmth or comfort. Nothing about it seemed like anything other than a vid screen.

"Or it could be someone from the future," Emily mused.

"If so, whoever left the 'reverse shadow' could be from the future too. That could mean there is an extra person wondering around … Have we heard anything from Butkus?" he asked.

"He says there's something wrong with his equipment. He keeps getting an invalid reading."

"What's that mean?"

Emily smiled humorlessly. "I asked him the same thing. He said something about contaminated samples."

"Two to one it's me." Roy's tone hid the tension they were both feeling as he voiced his fear.

"More like a thousand to one, seeing as how I'm not authorized to use the time machine." Emily stared at him. "What now? People will realize I didn't find anyone missing, and we don't exactly get illegal immigrants here."

"Gordon thinks it was a ghost."

Emily raised her eyebrows incredulously. "The mess? There ain't nothing ghostly about that. Does he think a ghost crapped out that mess? What the …?" Emily closed her mouth as she thought. "I hope he keeps that shit to himself. The last thing we need is him telling everyone some kind of moon-ghost is killing people. We'd be better off telling them about the time machine and getting court-martialed for it."

Roy's door alert sounded.

As soon as Roy said "Enter," Gordon pushed in faster than the door could move out of his way. He was holding something that looked like a gun with a slimy yellow popsicle shoved in the barrel. Emily sighed and started to leave.

"Wait, Emily." Roy stopped her before she could get out. "Okay, Gordon. Before you launch into another flurry of information I don't understand, explain the ghost thing to us again."

Gordon sighed, as though he knew this was a waste of time. "All right. According to the theory of supersymmetry, each particle has a superpartner …"

7

"Gordon," Roy interrupted, "I want to understand it, not ..."

"Okay! Okay, okay. Imagine a giant ballroom, with the whole far wall made of a giant mirror, so when you walk in, you spot your own reflection way over there.

"That's our universe. Except the mirror isn't just a reflection, it actually is the other half of our universe. But we can't walk over to the mirror, because it's here, all around us, already. When a collection of particles comes together here, a like collection comes together there, making a dark matter mirror image. Sort of. Actually it's more like the way ..."

"Gordon ..." Emily nearly growled at him.

"Well?" Gordon shrugged helplessly, still holding the strange device in his hands. "Did you ever play with magnets? Put one on top of a table and one on bottom, then move one to make the other move like magic?" He looked at them hopefully. "It's like that. When something on our side of the mirror moves around, the opposite something moves around on the other side. Okay. So. Now let's imagine the mirror isn't perfect.

"Imagine a boulder, here, that we smash into gravel. For some reason, the boulder over there sometimes smashes into gravel too, but sometimes it stays a boulder. We don't know why." He stopped and looked at them. "You realize I am really oversimplifying this, right?"

Emily's left eye twitched at him in annoyance.

"What we think, is that when matter here forms into what we call life," Gordon continued, "the dark matter there forms into a 'mirror image' of life: a spirit, or a ghost.

"The problem with the mirror image idea is that you think I am talking about your reflection over there. I'm not. I'm talking about your reflection being in the same place, at the same time, as you. So your spirit, your ghost, is always right where you are. Until you die. Then, sometimes, like the boulder that didn't turn to gravel, the spirit stays intact even though the body has fallen apart.

"Now this is where it gets really interesting." Gordon's eyes lit up. "Remember the magnet under the table? Well imagine the one on top gets smashed, but the bottom one doesn't." Gordon realized both Roy and Emily were glaring now, so he sped up his explanation, talking faster.

"So! The magnet on top was stopping the one on bottom from moving through the table. It was in the way. Now it's gone, and the one on bottom can move through the table to the top anytime it wants to. Perhaps some missing people have gone missing because their 'ghost' died and they were able to, somehow, wander over to the other side. And, vise-versa, ghosts wander over to our side." Gordon stopped, pleased with himself that he had been able to talk down to their level.

Emily looked ready to punch him.

"So, what you're saying," Roy stood up, casually placing himself between Emily and Gordon, "is that ghosts are actually from another dimension, and can come into ours anytime they want?"

Gordon frowned. "No, that's not what I said at all. I …" He wisely closed his mouth and thought for a moment. "Yes. I believe that is as good of a way of looking at it as you will ever … Ahem. Yes."

"I don't get it." Emily shook her head. "Why can they do that? And if they're anti-matter or dark matter or whatever, wouldn't they just explode in our universe?"

Gordon sighed. "There's something different about them. We believe the supersymmetry somehow gets broken. The particles change and …" He stopped at the looks on their faces. "I don't know. And I don't know why sometimes people see them and sometimes they don't. But," he held up his slimy yellow popsicle device. "I think we can now!"

"What is it?" Roy asked.

"I analyzed the data on the energy spike, and I think I have isolated the specific frequencies of the Higgsinos and stop squarks that …" Gordon shut his mouth again. He took a breath and then finished, "I think I can make a ghost glow so we can actually see it!" He grinned at the looks on their faces. "The moon was the perfect place to search, because there shouldn't be any ghosts here! Well. No more than three anyway. But that energy spike at three o'clock this morning gave me the clue I needed! I think I know what ghosts are, and I think I can use this to make them visible!" He held up his strange device excitedly.

17AUG52 17:58

"You can't be serious about this, Roy." Emily, for the first time since she had known him, stepped in Roy's path and physically stopped him. If it made Roy angry, he didn't show it.

"I have to use the time machine anyway. I use it every night.

9

These reports are the whole reason this base is up here on the moon. I might as well take a few minutes to find out what the hell happened. It won't be hard to do."

"They warned us about using the time machine. Unpredictable effects, accidentally killing yourself and all that. Remember? Besides, you know as well as I do, after what we found in the maintenance hall, stepping into that time machine could be a death sentence." Emily was on the verge of pleading with him, crossing a boundary their relationship had never known before.

"You mean I shouldn't go at all?" An incredulous tone crept into Roy's voice. "If I refuse to travel back in time and turn in this report, then what? They'll put you in command. And when you refuse to do it, they'll court martial you too."

"This assignment took us beyond that, Roy. You know as well as I do they'll kill us to keep their secrets safe."

"So, what do I do, Emily? If I go, I might die. If I don't go, they will 'court martial' me." Roy shook his head. "That would start with four years in the brig, up here on the moon, just to wait for a trial. That would be worse than a death sentence, and you know it. Besides, everyone on the base is scared shitless. We're the only ones who have any idea what it might be. All anyone else knows is that whatever it was that happened, it's life threatening—"

"Not on a global scale, it's not! And that's all our bosses care about. They're not going to forgive you for using their toy 'just this one time.'"

"You mean they will kill me."

"No, Roy, I mean us. Where you go, I follow. You know that. It was asinine of them to make me second in command with kill orders if you stepped out of line. I would follow you back into hell if you asked. Maybe even if you didn't ask." Emily fought back tears of emotion, embarrassed they would show like this after everything they had slogged through dry-eyed together. "If you choose to do this, I won't stop you, but goddamn it, you think it through first." Emily stared him hard in the eyes, not daring him, not defying him, but asking for his respect.

"They stuck us up here on the moon with the time machine for a reason," Roy held his hands wide. "Haven't you ever thought about why?"

"Yeah, so we could travel back in time and warn them if they blew themselves up! We'll still be floating up here."

"That's their story. I think the 'warnings' about how you can accidentally kill yourself are a load of crap. I think their machine has already been used to make the world the way they want it, and they're afraid of someone taking that away. I bet we're on the moon just so we can't do that.

"I mean, so what if you can go back to yesterday and change it? You're trapped on the friggin' moon! What are you going to do, make your five year stint even longer by living through a few extra days? Skip ahead to the end and hope no one notices you were gone? You can't call home without going through their channels. There's no privacy, no chance to send any messages. I bet every time the machine gets used, it sends a warning back in time to them to let them know someone messed with it.

"I'm going to be using it for a regularly scheduled transmission. No one will ever know if I spent that extra five minutes picking up something I knocked over or just plain pickin' my ass."

Emily sighed. "I don't like knowing that ... *mess* in the hall is probably you."

"I'm not going back to last night. I'm going back three months. And I will only be there long enough to send the report, and plant these in that vent." He pointed to a pinhole camera and the gun-like ghost device he had gotten from Gordon. "We need to know what happened. The more we look at this, the more it looks like a murder, and odds are good it was one of us who died. We need to figure this out or we'll both go crazy wondering."

Roy smiled at her reassuringly. "This trip will take an extra three minutes on my end, nothing will change here. You'll never even know I was gone."

Emily got a strange look on her face. "Has that ever happened before? Have you come back, and we didn't even know? I mean ... have you come back and we were ... different?"

"What? No!" Roy laughed. "How could anything possibly cause that?"

"Well, what happens if something does affect us?"

"In that case," Roy grinned at her, "they should have already sent up a notice to stop me in one of these reports I send them from the future."

"Unless they wanted you dead. Why haven't you sent a warning to protect yourself? Maybe you don't come back." Emily stopped, fighting back tears, embarrassed they would show.

"If I didn't come back, I'm sure you would have sent yourself a warning." Roy picked up the pinhole camera and ghost gun thing. "I'm going to plant these in that vent so we can see what happened. I'm going to send their report, and I will be back in thirty seconds your time. Then we'll go together and get these back out of the vent and see what's on the camera."

"I don't suppose it would do any good to remind you that video surveillance is illegal?"

"Maybe they could tack that on to my list of crimes and get permission to use a dull needle when they kill me."

Out of arguments, Emily stepped back as Roy tapped the concealed pressure plate that moved his desk and opened the secret door hidden behind it. He gave her an exaggerated wink as he entered and shut the door.

"Be careful, Roy," she whispered to herself.

She turned to watch the chronometer on Roy's desk. It was going to be a long thirty seconds. Her communicator beeped and she tapped her wrist absently. "Yeah?"

"I can't raise Roy on his com." It was Butkus' voice.

"He's indisposed. He'll be available in a couple of minutes," Emily answered.

"Have him call me as soon as he can," Butkus' tinny voice echoed in the small office. "I've done every test I can. I even switched machines. There's no doubt about it. The DNA all over that hallway is Roy's."

Emily hung her head. It wasn't a surprise, but it had been better not knowing.

10NOV52 02:01

Roy stuck the tiny camera in his pocket and shifted Gordon's slimy ghost device to his other hand as he opened the secret door from the inside. The room lights were dimmed. He was never in his office between two and four in the morning, that way he would never run into himself.

He expected the office to be vacant. Instead, he found Emily sitting at his desk—dead with a bullet hole in her head.

Stunned, he stared at her slack grey face for a long time. He leaned against his desk to steady himself and gather his thoughts. He was sure Emily hadn't done this to herself, and not just because there was no gun in sight. There wouldn't be. They hadn't brought any to the moon with them. Who would have done this? And why? Roy felt weak and his head spun with questions.

Eventually, his eyes wandered to the chronometer. He hadn't gone three months into the past. He had gone nearly three months into the future.

How had he ended up in the future instead of the past? Who would have taken the time to build a projectile weapon? Why was Emily's body still here? She had obviously been dead for a few days. Didn't anyone know? Maybe the mess in the hallway really had been a murder. Had the same person now killed Emily?

He started to head out of his office, to go find who had done this, but then he remembered *when* he was—this was the future.

Things didn't have to be this way. Emily didn't have to be dead. He could just go back, right now, right to when he came from, and prevent this from happening.

Hurriedly he stepped back through the secret door. As he punched the buttons to take him back, he was startled by the glowing form of Emily's ghost drifting in after him.

17AUG52 18:05

Emily couldn't wait any longer. Roy hadn't come back in thirty seconds, and that meant he wasn't coming back. Whatever had happened to him, she was going to prevent it. She stepped into the machine and set it to repeat so she could follow him. Nothing happened. It was set to respond only to Roy.

She grit her teeth in frustration. She had to get to an emergency override panel and give herself access. Earth would be notified immediately by the use of the panel, but if Roy hadn't come back, it was because he couldn't, and she intended to find him.

The nearest override panel was surrounded by people who all looked up at the sight of her, hoping she had news about what had happened in the maintenance hallway. She smiled politely and shook her head, moving on towards another secret panel. There were people working in the area around that panel, too. It took her three tries before she found one without people around to complicate matters. It took her only a moment to give herself access.

10NOV52 02:12

Roy stared at the ghost hovering before his eyes. It was Emily, of that he had no doubts.

"Emily?" he asked hesitantly. The apparition didn't show any signs that it heard him. He reached out and tried to touch it, but his hand passed through. He felt nothing. "Emily?" It didn't respond.

Roy opened the time machine's door and stepped out, warily eyeing Emily's glowing visage. He held up Gordon's device and waved it at the apparition. The figure brightened and became more visible as it came closer. He flicked the device off and on and the form disappeared and reappeared. As he moved away, the ghost followed him like a luminescent shadow.

Roy realized he was still in the room with Emily's body. He glanced at the chronometer again. He hadn't changed time. The time machine hadn't worked.

The office door hissed open and Roy barely had time to jump out of the way as bullets ripped through the space he had been standing in. The bullets passed through Emily's ghost without effect, but the sight of the shining apparition stopped the shooter in his tracks.

Roy did a leg sweep on the man in the moment of distraction. Within seconds, Roy had him disarmed and unconscious. Roy examined his assailant. A general in combat uniform. He had probably been sent to replace Roy as Commander of Luna Base.

Roy began to understand what must have happened. Earth had sent soldiers to Luna. They had locked him out of the time machine and executed Emily for treason.

By jumping into the future, not only had he not returned in thirty seconds, he hadn't returned at all. Emily must have done something to try to save him. Likely, she had tried to send a message back in time to warn herself.

"Is he the one that killed you, Emily?" Roy asked the ghost as he considered snapping the man's neck.

Her ghost didn't respond. He decided there was no point in killing the man if he could go back in time and make sure this never happened. Emily's ghost followed him back into the time machine as he used the general's clearance badge to reactivate it.

17AUG52 18:13

Memories of the mess in the hallway haunted Emily; she had to prevent that from happening to Roy. She stepped into the machine and set it to follow Roy, but then she hesitated.

Think smart, she told herself. Make a battle plan. She could travel ahead, find out what happened to Roy, and then come back forearmed with knowledge. That was the true power of a time machine.

She reset the destination four years ahead, a week prior to their departure from Luna. She would check the computer files, find out what had happened, and then she would know how to prevent it.

When she stepped out of the time machine, she was surprised to find Roy's office empty, devoid of all furniture. There was no computer to check. Where was everything? What had happened?

Caught in a moment of indecision, she was startled by two armed soldiers entering the room. Fortunately, they were surprised by her as well.

She took the first one down quickly, but the second one drew his gun and fired wildly at her. She had no choice but to use the first soldier's weapon to defend herself. Two quick shots and the man slumped to the floor, dead.

This is bad, she told herself. Bad, bad, bad. Why were there armed soldiers on Luna Base?

As soon as she started the thought process, she realized she had left Luna Base without a commander by jumping into the future. There wouldn't be any answers here. The only thing she would find here would be a 'court martial'. She turned and re-entered the time machine.

17AUG52 18:15

Roy found himself back to within minutes of when he had left, but not the time he had set it for. Emily wasn't in the office. Her ghost seemed to lose interest in him and wandered off, passing through the doors as though they weren't there.

Why wasn't the time machine functioning properly? Why was he ending up in the wrong times?

Roy realized the answer as soon as he sat it down on his desk.

Gordon's ghost gun. Roy took a deep breath and blew out his frustration in a huff as he looked at the strange piece of equipment. Whatever the gun did, it must somehow affect the time machine too.

Irritated, he shut it off. He didn't want to ever see Emily's ghost again anyway. It brought back the memory of her physical body's pale dead face, with the trickle of dried blood coming from the hole in her forehead. Seeing her like that was something he had feared and dared not imagined for years.

"Emily? Are you there?" He called her communicator. When she didn't answer, tightness began forming in his chest. She must have gone after him when he hadn't returned fast enough. If so, then why wasn't she back already? Where would she have gone?

All of that blood at the end of the service corridor. And no one missing—except Emily. She hadn't been missing then, but she was missing now. And she had access to a time machine. Had the thousand to one longshot that it was her in the hallway come in? Maybe, maybe not. But if she used the time machine to go looking for him, there was only one place she would think she could find him.

Roy moved back into the time machine and set it for the night before.

Unseen, Emily's ghost silently followed him.

10SEP56 02:08

Emily stood shaking with frustration inside the time machine. It wouldn't activate. They must have removed her authorization.

She exited the machine and began pacing the office. She had to do something. Could she make it back to one of the access panels without being seen? She doubted it. Someone probably heard those shots and would be coming to investigate soon.

The soldier she had disarmed groaned. She glanced down at him and realized he wasn't just a soldier. The rank on his combat uniform was that of a general. Emily quickly went through his pockets and pulled out his clearance card.

The sound of footfalls carried through the door. She had to hurry.

Her breathing was loud in her ears she re-entered the little chamber and swiped the clearance card. There was only one place she could think of Roy wouldn't have been able to come back from: that damned bloody hallway.

Butkus had said it was Roy's DNA all over that hallway. That's where Roy had to end up. She would just have to get there first.

Without Gordon's ghost device, she was unable to see Roy's ghost enter the chamber with her.

17AUG52 02:56

Relief flooded tears into Emily's eyes as she rounded the corner into the dead end service hallway. Roy was already there, leaning against the wall and looking bored. She had made it in time!

He stood up straight and grinned when he saw her.

Emily, trying to regain her composure, resisted the urge to run to him. She started towards him, not sure what to say, and then Roy's ghost appeared beside her. It startled Emily and she jumped away from it. Dimly luminescent at first, it grew brighter as it drifted towards Roy.

Confusion crossed Roy's face as the ghost approached. "Is that my ghost? Yours was just here, too. It went through that wall." Roy pointed his thumb without looking away from the specter. It picked up speed as it neared him, jumping the last few feet impossibly quick.

Roy's body exploded into a red cloud.

Stunned, Emily fell to her knees. Aerosolized particulate made the air hazy and pink. "Roy?" she asked in a small voice. There was no answer. Droplets formed and fell like rain. The odor of humidity and blood filled her senses.

Emily tried to regain control of herself, crawling to the wall for support. Haltingly, she got to her feet and stumbled toward where Roy had been. She had witnessed his death, but she had no idea what she had seen.

Had that really been Roy's ghost?

Was it a secret weapon from Earth? Some kind of failsafe to make sure Roy didn't misuse the time machine?

She had to change this. How? How could she change it? She could lock him out from the time machine! She could use the emergency access panel before he left, deny his access to the time machine until she could explain it to him!

She was surprised by a glowing image of herself floating through the wall Roy had pointed to. It seemed confused, disoriented.

It floated in a circle around the mess, and then began drifting towards her.

Emily panicked and ran for the time machine. She had to get to it before that thing caught up with her! She had to set things right, she had to save Roy.

She scrambled into Roy's office, and hurriedly tried to set the time machine to take her back to before Roy left, back to when she could stop all of this from happening.

17AUG52 09:39

Roy's door alert sounded. As soon as Roy said "Enter," Gordon pushed in faster than the door could move out of his way. He was holding something that looked like a gun with a slimy yellow popsicle shoved in the barrel. Emily sighed and started to leave.

"Wait, Emily," Roy stopped her before she could get out. "Okay, Gordon. Before you launch into another flurry of information I don't understand, explain the ghost thing to us one more time."

Gordon sighed, as though he knew this was a waste of time. "All right. According to the theory of supersymmetry, each particle has a superpartner …"

A strange whumping sound from the hidden door behind his desk interrupted him.

Gordon raised his eyebrows and looked questioningly from Roy to Emily. They both stared at him blankly for a moment before Roy finally asked "Can you excuse us for a few minutes, Gordon?"

Gordon hesitated, and then retreated from the office.

"I would guess that's our evidence someone has been monkeying around with the time machine." Emily stood up and walked around the desk.

Roy tapped the concealed pressure plate that moved his desk and opened the secret door hidden behind it. A rush of bloody fluids poured out from under the door as it opened. The moist air and fetid smell filled the small office.

17AUG52 11:38

Roy's communicator beeped again. "They just won't give up,

will they?" he grunted as he stood up from where he had been cleaning the mess off his office floor.

"I guess not." Emily's voice was muffled. She had tied a t-shirt over her nose and mouth as she mopped.

"I'm busy!" Roy growled into his wrist. "It will have to wait!"

"We know you have a time machine in there. Open up." It was Gordon's voice.

Roy shut off the communicator angrily. "How in the hell does he know that?"

"Who cares? Open the door. We need the air and he can help clean up."

Roy thought about it for a moment and then sighed. "Enter."

The door slid open and Butkus and Gordon both winced as the smell hit them. Gordon held up his strange ghost gun and waved it around. He seemed disappointed when nothing happened.

"I found these in that vent." Butkus looked apologetic as he held up the pinhole camera and the twin to the device Gordon held in his hand.

"Yeah … That kind of gave away the whole time machine thing." Gordon pointed at the ghost-gun in Butkus' hand with the one in his own. "I only made one of these, and no one else knows how. Yet there are two of them."

"Not to mention what the camera caught," Butkus added.

Gordon held up his PPD for them to see and touched the screen. An image of Roy's face filled the screen. "Roy. Emily," the somber face addressed them, "this is that warning you always told yourself you'd send back to yourself. Don't do anything except what you are supposed to do, or it all goes to shit. And by the way—"

Gordon tapped the screen and the image jumped to an empty hallway.

"Hey!" Emily "Why'd you do that? Go back!"

"Gordon," Butkus admonished, "they need to see that. It's important."

Gordon sighed and tapped the screen again. Roy's face reappeared.

"… all goes to shit. And by the way, Gordon's damned ghost machine thing works but it screws up the time machine. You don't end up where you were trying to go. And that makes everything go to shit, too."

The recorded visage looked as though it wanted to say more but it didn't. Instead the video jumped and showed Roy's hand and face as he placed the camera and Gordon's ghost-gun into the vent and replaced the cover.

Gordon tapped the PPD screen a few times. "There is about a day's worth of nothing recoded on here we need to skip," he explained. After a couple more taps, an image of Roy appeared in the hallway.

"You just stand there for about an hour," Gordon said as he skipped more video. "And then …"

"Is that my ghost?" Roy's recorded voice asked. "Yours was just here, too. It went through that wall." A moment later a blur of light entered the picture and Roy vanished, replaced by a red mist.

"Roy?" Emily's shaky voice could barely be heard on the recording. A glowing image of Emily came out of the wall and drifted in a circle before moving out of the picture.

Gordon shut off the PPD. "That's it."

"What the …" Emily's mouth worked up and down silently as she looked away from the blank PPD.

"That was a ghost," Gordon informed her. "I believe we have just witnessed a new type of energy being released, something along the lines of a matter/anti-matter explosion. I assume that the mess you are currently cleaning up is a result of the same catastrophic mistake."

Gordon stood up straight and tucked his PPD under his arm. "This is what happens when you give big kid toys to the little kids. *Of course* the energies that would make time travel possible would be disrupted by one of these." He held up his ghost device. "If you would have seen fit to share the knowledge that there was a time machine on this base …"

Roy interrupted him by handing him a mop. "While you are cleaning up this mess, I will be researching regulations, looking for a loophole that says you don't have to be executed for knowing there is a time machine on Luna Base."

Roy turned and stalked out the door leaving Gordon dismayed.

"You, too." Emily handed her mop to Butkus and followed Roy.

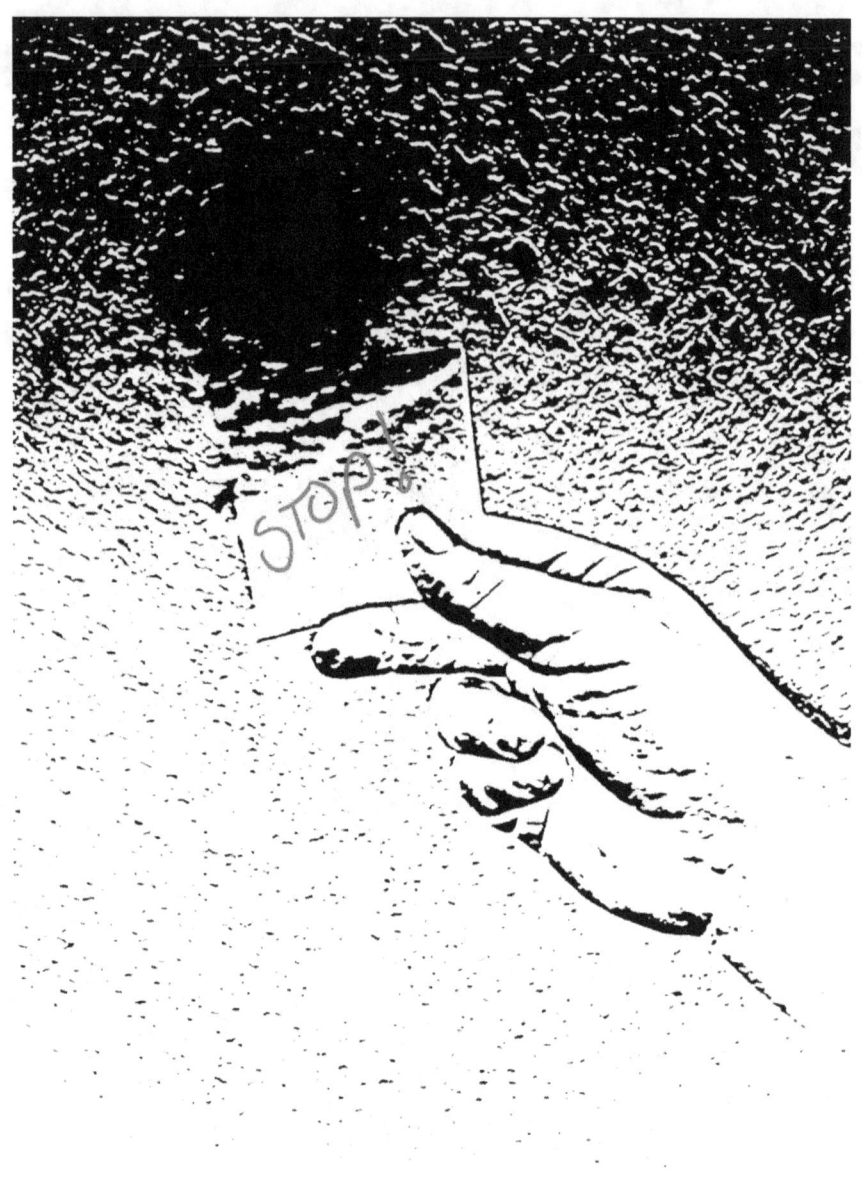

Just in Time for a Celebration

Peter stood up from the tangled mess of wires that had grown into a small hill in the middle of his lab. The light on his soldering gun went out as he released the trigger but a small wisp of smoke came off the tip and remained hanging in the air under the fluorescent lights. He put one hand to his back and leaned backwards to stretch out the pain settling there after the last couple of hours of crawling around inspecting the myriad wires and connections.

He let his tired arms drop to his sides as he stood straight again and a grin spread wide across his face. Today was the day. No ifs, ands, or buts about it. No wondering, no worrying, and no doubts.

What a liberating feeling, he thought with a smile. After all those late night discussions with his brother about free will and determinism, and Peter himself always arguing for free will, it was so odd that today's events were predetermined and yet he still felt so ... free, so unburdened by the fear of failure or doubt.

He stepped out of the pile of wires and placed the soldering gun on the cluttered workbench. Wiping at an itch on his forehead with the back of his hand, he called his brother's name out loud. "Cyril!"

Peter hadn't seen Cyril all day, but he wasn't worried about it. He put his hand in his pocket and fingered the note he had found on his bathroom mirror this morning. He had also found a little box wrapped in a golden bow on his workbench. The box had contained his new watch. A present from himself.

He glanced at the timepiece on his wrist. It fit as if it had been made for him. Which obviously it had—it had his name engraved on the back. Cleverly designed to look like an old watch, he was sure it was some sort of future technology. He hadn't figured out how to use it yet, but he knew it was a gift from the future. A present to himself from the future.

He couldn't wait to show his brother! Proof! He had proof! He raised his fist with the watch on it in triumph as his grin broadened again.

"Cyril!" he called again, this time sticking his head out into the hall. When no reply came, Peter left his lab and headed for Cyril's.

Cyril's lab was the next door down the hall but was hundred foot walk, as the adjacent rooms were both large. When Peter reached his brother's lab he found it empty.

Unlike Peter's room, Cyril's was immaculate. Every tool in its place, every stainless steel counter and white cupboard door wiped down to a shine, and every window blind cracked the exact same amount. Although Cyril was obviously not in his lab at this moment, the cleanliness was not an indication of when Cyril had last been there.

Only one thing stood out. A small box wrapped with a golden ribbon tied in a bow sat in the middle of Cyril's workbench. It looked just like the one Peter had found his watch in. Curious, he crossed the room and picked it up. A simple nametag had Cyril's name printed on it. Peter put it back smiling to himself. His future-self must have left this here for his brother to find.

He considered peeking and seeing what it was, but if his future self had wanted his past self to open it, it would have been left with the other. Not to mention it wouldn't have Cyril's name on it.

Peter shrugged to himself and headed back to his own lab. "Your loss, Cyril..." he muttered out loud as a wry grin crept across his face in anticipation.

He entered his lab rubbing his hands together in eager anticipation, feeling giddy, and thinking about the future of the past. He checked the platform of the time machine's portal one last time, for safety's sake, even though he knew nothing would go wrong.

Resisting the impulse to skip, he hurried to the power box and connected the breaker switches. The hum of the equipment coming to life added to Peter's own energy as he scurried over to the computer monitor. He tapped his foot impatiently, yet with a big smile on his face, feeling like a mad scientist as he waited for the program to boot up.

A wispy smell of smoke caught his attention. Not the acrid smoke of the solder he'd had in his nose all morning, rather a warmer, woody smoke.

Peter sniffed at the air, his smile fading. Could something have gone wrong? Surely not! Not today of all days! He had a note in his pocket from his future self, telling him today was the day he succeeded!

Confused, and a little worried, Peter began sniffing and looking around the lab. A faint trace of smoke pulled him back towards the portal where he expected to open a hole through time in just minutes. A small yellow note was on the floor, smoke still coming off its edges.

Peter picked it up, confused, and read it. It had one hastily scrawled word on it: *Stop!*

The note was still warm in Peter's fingers as his face hardened in thought. Had he sent this to himself from the future? Had something gone wrong? That didn't make any sense. He already had a note in his pocket from his future self!

Maybe there was something he had overlooked. Something he had to fix before he could succeed. That must be it.

He ran back to the power box to turn off the power just in time to see another smoking note hit the floor. He grabbed it quickly, reading: *Not this!*

"Crap!" he yelled at himself, unsure what to do. "Crap! Crap! Crap!"

He ran back to the computer just in time to see a smoldering note appear out of thin air and waft down to the keyboard. He snatched at it without hesitation. *Not the computer!*

Peter hesitated, stalled by confusion. It must be in the wires he had just finished connecting! He had been too cocky and overconfident with the note in his pocket guaranteeing his success and he had messed something up.

Just as he reached where the pile of connections met in the middle of his lab, another note appeared in the air and began to fall. *Give up!*

Give up? "Never!" Peter snarled at himself, crumpling the note and throwing it across the room. It bounced off the air and landed back at Peter's feet with a small skittering sound.

The look on Peter's face must have been too much for Cyril, as he finally let loose a snort, followed by a chuckle and finally outright guffawing.

Peter looked around confused. "Cyril?"

Cyril's head appeared, floating in the air. "You hit me right in the eye!"

Realization crossed Peter's face. "You solved your invisibility problem!"

Cyril grinned and nodded, his disembodied head bobbing like a helium balloon on a string.

"You were dropping those notes? And I didn't even know you were in here? How did you light them on fire without me catching you? Does it block UV and IR too? How were you so quiet?" Peter's questions gushed at his brother until Cyril finally hugged him to contain Peter's excitement.

"And you? Were you really ready to test your time machine?" Cyril finally asked without answering the other questions.

"Yeah! Look! I left myself a note on my bathroom mirror this..." Peter's face fell as he pulled the note out and looked at it again. *Today's the day!*

"You wrote this, didn't you?" Peter asked looking at the handwriting he now realized wasn't his.

Cyril looked away, abashed. "I snuck in and put it there. I didn't realize you would think it was from ... well ... you. I just wanted to show off how I could sneak around in my new suit."

"What about the watch?" Peter remembered.

Cyril looked at Peter's watch and raised his eyebrows. "What about it?"

"Ha! See!" Peter yelled excitedly, waving his wrist in the air.

"See what? Mom told me she was sending our birthday presents to the lab to save money on shipping."

"She did?" Peter's face fell. Peter and Cyril had been born a year apart and Mom usually sent both of their presents at the same time. That explained the present in Cyril's lab, too. Peter sighed. It hurt to think he hadn't written the notes or sent the watch, but he stifled his own disappointment, trying to focus on his brother's success.

"How does it do in direct sunlight? Have you found any limitations?" Peter asked as he ran a hand down Cyril's invisible arm, feeling something like plastic covered with silk.

The smile returned to Cyril's face. "Come on, I'll show you!" He grabbed Peter with an invisible hand and headed out the door and into a crowded hallway full of Peters.

"Surprise!" a chorused yell came from dozens of voices, all the same. Four of the Peters in front waved a 'Congratulations Cyril!' banner in front of the crowd.

"Holy crap!" breathed Cyril in surprise as he and Peter nearly fell over each other. Peter held on to Cyril's invisible arm for balance as Cyril's head bounced frantically around in the air.

The crowd of doppelgängers burst out laughing. Two Peters on step ladders unfurled another banner with the words 'I just wanted to show off how I could sneak around!'

Peter held on tight to Cyril for support as he realized all of the people he was looking at were … himself.

"It works!" Peter yelled in excitement.

"Hell, yeah it works!" About half of the Peters in the hall answered him back in unison.

Peter grabbed for Cyril's other arm, missing twice because it was invisible, and pulled him around, dancing in a circle in excitement. "It works! It works!" he shouted elatedly at his brother's floating head.

An air horn cut through the noise and all of the Peters turned to look behind them. Seemingly out of thin air, a banquet table appeared, loaded with cakes with sparklers.

As one, dozens of Cyrils unmasked themselves and became floating heads as they removed the hoods from their invisibility suits. A banner unfurled from the front of the table reading: 'The Cake Is Not A Lie!'

The Peters began clapping and cheering their brothers' coup.

Peter and Cyril stood silently in the doorway, Peter's arms still hugging the invisible form of his brother. With wide eyes, they looked at each other. "I'm a bit overwhelmed." Cyril confided.

"And how!" Peter breathlessly nodded back.

"Come eat cake!" A few of the Cyrils' floating heads shouted in unison and then laughed at each other.

Peter and Cyril found each other trying hard to not lose each other in the crowd of their other selves, instinctually feeling different from the others somehow. "This sure is a lot of … us-es" Cyril commented, the word not comfortable in his mouth.

"You's and me's?" Peter offered weakly, watching all of the heads with his brother's face bobbing and weaving through the crowd of men who looked just like himself.

Peter found a piece of cake on a plate shoved into his hands by another Peter with a twinkling, knowing look in his eye. This Peter actually looked a little different, a little older maybe. He whispered, "You'll figure it out … in time." Then he winked and stepped back into the crowd, blending instantly.

Peter smiled at where his other-self had stood. "At least one of me has the decency to drop hints about the future," he murmured to Cyril. At least he *thought* it was his Cyril.

Peter looked around the room and realized it was oddly quiet for so many people. Peters ate cake next to floating Cyril heads who's mouths seemed to magically receive bites of cake from levitating plates and forks, but there was very little talking.

Of course! What is there to talk about to yourself? How do you have idle chit chat with someone who is thinking the same thing you are. It's like talking in a hall of mirrors. They had nothing new to say to each other, even if they were all Cyrils and himself. Himselfs? Himselves?

"We are going to have to invent new words…" He told the Cyril head hovering to his left and received a nod of assent in return.

"Okay, Peter!" One of the Cyrils stood up on a chair. At least Peter thought he stood on a chair. It actually looked as though Cyril's head had just floated ten feet up into the air. "Although this is the best company I've ever kept …"

All of the Peters laughed, but none of the Cyrils did. Peter realized all of the Cyrils must have already thought of that joke.

"Wow! Tough crowd!" the Cyril on the chair continued. This elicited a chuckle from a few of the Cyrils who hadn't thought of that yet. "Anyway. Um, Peter? Can you send me back now? I couldn't figure out how."

"Hear! Hear!" chorused the Cyrils as they invisibly raised forks and plates into the air.

Laughter filled the room from the Peters and one of them stepped up on a chair next to the Cyril on the chair. "Okay, Cyril! Cyrils … All of you! Look at your watches!"

Plates and forks levitated in strange directions as all of the Cyrils began pulling off their left gloves and adding floating hands to the crowd. The Peters all chuckled at the sight.

"We need you to line up in order of time shift. Those who were first to go through the portal on that end," Peter on the chair pointed to a wall, "those last on this end. If you know you were the first or the last, get to the ends so everyone can line up in order."

Heads bobbed and bounced as the Cyrils moved around to

comply. Apparently there was no need to give instructions to the Peters as all of them but one began moving along with the Cyrils.

"Oh, there you are," said Cyril with an air of smarmy indifference as his head sidled up to Peter's shoulder. "I'd wondered where you had gotten off to."

"Just another face in the crowd," Peter grinned at him.

"Yeah, me too," Cyril smirked.

After a few minutes of shuffling, the line settled down, matching Peters to Cyrils with only three Cyrils left unmatched.

"Don't worry!" One of the Peters called out to them. "We'll get you back too!"

"It doesn't work!" A Peter called out with panic in his voice. His face was pinched as he fiddled with his wristwatch. It was the same as the one Peter had found this morning.

Peter's heart sank as he saw all of the other Peters get the same lost look on their faces as they tried the devices on their wrists. Realization seemed to pass over the faces of the Peters in a wave and they all ended up looking at the first Peter and Cyril standing alone by the cake.

Peter looked down at his own watch. It was just as functional, or not, as it had been this morning. Then he realized that wasn't why they were all looking at him …

"Oh, crap." Peter sighed as he realized what all the other Peters must have already.

"What?" Cyril demanded, echoed by the voices of several of his other selves.

"They broke the causality continuation."

"I don't know what that means," frustration tinted Cyril's voice.

"Who was first Peter?" Peter raised his voice and asked.

All of the Peters glanced around sheepishly. One reluctantly raised his hand.

"When did you go through?" Peter asked his no-longer future self.

"Right after Cyril got done showing me his suit. About ten minutes ago…" he answered looking at his watch.

All of the Cyrils' eyes were on the Peter talking except the Cyril by the Peter asking. He was intent on the one Peter he felt sure was actually *his* brother. "What does that mean?" he asked hoarsely.

"It means they changed their own past. They stopped me from going through ten minutes ago, and now I am no longer them from their memories. They are no longer future versions of me."

"So? Why can't they go back?"

Looks of panic were starting to spread across the Cyrils' floating heads, mirroring their brothers.

"Because their past no longer exits," Peter waived his hands in frustration. "They can't go back to a place that never was …"

"So they are all stuck here? Now?"

"No. They can go wherever they want—except where they came from."

"They can go back to right when they left!"

Peter shook his head. "They already came back to when they left from! They came from here! Now!"

Cyril's head rotated to face Peter, his jaw slackened. "You didn't build a time machine, you built a cloning machine!"

Muttering and exasperated sighs filled the room as Peters rubbed their foreheads and Cyrils began to realize they were stuck.

"Okay, I've got it," Cyril told Peter. "Go get in your time machine, go back, and stop this from ever happening!"

Peter sighed. "If I go do that, you will still be standing here with all of them, but no me. I will just change my past again, not theirs, and I will still be standing right next to myself like a clone."

"Send a note?" Cyril asked hopefully.

"And what? Same thing. A me in the past will make a different choice, one I don't remember, one that is not the one I made, and that 'me' will split off to become his own timeline, just like they did." Peter waved at the crowd where small groups were forming and having very similar discussions.

"Oh, this hurts my head," Cyril moaned, his one visible hand floating up to his temple.

"I'm glad you've still got your sense of humor," Peter commented wryly.

"Oh, ha ha. Well at least you now know why your future self never came back and visited you like you always promised yourself you would." Cyril gave Peter a disgusted look.

Peter nodded. "That's for sure. No. Wait. I still could. As long as I don't interfere with myself like … these me's did."

"How would you be sure you didn't interfere? It would have to be something you already remember happening to you, and you have no memories of ever interacting with yourself. Do you?"

Peter shook his head, too frustrated to make the obvious joke.

"No. Besides that would create a paradox."

Cyril laughed out loud causing several of the others to glance his way. "This isn't a paradox?"

Peter shrugged. "I guess it would have the same results as this, but *that* me would be the only one who didn't show up here."

They sat in silence for a moment listening to the murmuring of their other selves. Finally Peter stood up. "Who was the last Peter and the last Cyril?"

One of the Peters stood up and one of Cyril heads waved a disembodied hand around.

"No memories of this? This is a first for both of you?"

They both nodded.

"Too much to hope, I guess ..." Peter muttered resignedly and sat back down.

A watch alarm began beeping and one of the Cyrils checked his wrist and shut it off. After a few minutes, another Cyril silenced his watch. When the third alarm went off, the Cyril next to Peter asked, "Why don't I have one of those?"

"That must be what's in the present in your lab." Peter answered.

"I didn't know there was a present in my lab."

"Well, your past, or future, or whatever, got changed too. Did anyone ever tell you talking to a disembodied head is pretty disconcerting?"

"No, no one has ever mentioned that before."

"Well, let me be the first ..." Peter's voice trailed off.

"I know that look!" Cyril said excitedly and several other Cyrils looked up, hopeful.

"We are the first! Cyril! You and me!" Peter's excitement rose. He saw the confusion on his brother's face. "Look at you! Just try! Ha! You invented invisibility on the same day I invented time travel! That's why no one has ever *seen* a time traveler. We must have always used them in conjunction!"

"That's great, Peter." Cyril spread his hands wide. "How does that help us now?"

"We have already traveled back in time and visited ourselves; we just didn't *see* us when we were there!"

"I am so lost, Peter."

"The watches! Time travel! How obvious of a clue does it have to be? Come on!" Peter got up and started running back to Cyril's lab. Cyril followed as the others watched them go. A few looked as though they might follow, but one of the Peters called for attention and asked if maybe they could all pool their thoughts for a solution.

Peter arrived at Cyril's lab and tore open the present before Cyril could catch up. Inside was the watch all of the other Cyrils were wearing. He turned it over eagerly, examining everything about it.

"Well?" Cyril asked as he caught up, head and hand floating through the doorway.

"Nothing. It looks used, and a lot like mine, but I don't see anything that might help." Peter handed it to Cyril.

Cyril turned the watch over in his visible hand, looking at it, and then put it on. "Perfect fit!" he grinned at Peter, then saw look of hopelessness settling across Peter's countenance. "I guess this is why we need time police," Cyril muttered.

"It wouldn't do any good." Peter mumbled dejectedly.

"Why not?"

"You can't change anyone's past except your own anyway."

Cyril made a face at Peter. "You've always said that, but look at what just happened."

"Yeah. I changed my own past. I mean, the future me's changed their pasts, which changed my future." Peter frowned. "You're right. It's not possible!" The excitement came back into Peter's eyes. "It can't be happening! There is no way!"

"What? Slow down! I'm not following." Cyril grabbed Peter with an invisible hand and pulled him back.

"When I asked if any of the others had any memories of this, they all said no!"

"So?"

"So! So that means the first one got all of the others before there ever was a party!"

"Peter! I don't understand!"

"Look! When did I—would I have started going through the time machine to set up the party?"

"Right after I would have taken you outside to show you my suit works perfect in any light," Cyril answered.

"Right. So I go through the machine to where? To my past? I would remember if I had pulled myself out of the past to come here!"

"So you grabbed future selves?"

"I would have to, right? But I couldn't have!"

"Why?"

"They just got done saying they couldn't go back to when they came from, right? Because they broke the causality. So every time the first me went into the future to get another me, that new me would have to have a memory of the party, or another causality would have been broken and none of them could ever have come back to the party! They, I, whatever, would have changed their personal past and erased it, so that future could not have been there either!"

"Oh, my God, Peter. You have hurt my head so much." Cyril's forehead contorted strangely as he massaged it with his invisible hand.

"Come on!" Peter pulled his brother along. "There is trickery afoot! They aren't real! They can't be!"

"They weren't." A voice from behind stopped them. "They were advanced holograms."

Peter and Cyril turned to face the empty lab. A floating head appeared as an invisibility hood was removed. This time it was Peter's face instead of Cyril's wearing the invisibility suit. An older Peter's face.

Peter narrowed his eyes. "You're …"

"The one who handed you the cake," Older Peter nodded. "And I actually am you. And this is the first time I have ever come back in time to talk to myself, so don't bother trying to remember any other times. I didn't keep my promise to myself, to you, to come back and drop hints, or whatever."

Cyril eyed him cautiously. "You are now. Why?"

"The party?" Older Peter's head bobbed as he gestured with his nose towards the hallway. "That was what I had wanted to happen." His mouth set in a thin line. "What really happened was I time jumped once, back in time, to get another version of myself, and broke the continuation of causality. I cloned myself, basically. Or to be more accurate, I turned myself into a clone. When we, the other Peter and I tried to time jump again, we couldn't. At least not to where we were trying to.

"I only jumped backwards the one time before I realized it would get really complicated trying to see how many other me's I could squeeze out of the ten minute window I had rashly given myself to pull from. So we, the other Peter and I, decided to jump ahead a little to get more of us." Old Peter eyes were distant as memories played where only he could see them. He paused and sighed, trying to figure out how to explain.

"When you jump to your own future, you aren't there. You haven't written it yet. To the rest of the world, you simply vanished when you stepped into the portal, never to be seen or heard of again until you step out. When you jump to your own past, you break causality, and effectively clone yourself. You erase your past and can never go back."

The younger Peter spoke up, almost afraid to ask his question. "So why are you here, in the past, breaking causality again?"

Older Peter must have wiped at a tear in his eye with an invisible hand as his cheek dented next to his nose and rippled outward. "I ruined my life. Your life," he pointed at Cyril, realized his hand was invisible and took off his gloves.

"My existence ruined your life, Cyril, and I can never forgive myself. So I am changing my past, splitting myself off one more time, so you can start anew. Without me there to ruin it."

"What happened? How can I avoid it?" Peter asked, concern weighing down his brow.

"Hopefully, we have already avoided it," Older Peter smiled wanly. "When I cloned myself ... Well, as egocentric as it is, we became best friends, the other Peter and I. Thing One and Thing Two we called each other, always calling ourselves One and the other Two, of course," he chuckled without humor. "We became self-absorbed, with each other."

Cyril raised his eyebrows.

"Not like that. We just didn't ... need anyone else. Why do you need someone else when you have someone who agrees with every idea you have, who jumps in and helps whole-heartedly, who wants exactly what you want?"

"So what happened?" Peter asked again.

"We finally changed enough to have a difference of opinion. And we fought horribly. Domestic squabbles are spilled milk in comparison. Cyril tried to help. He tried to fix things between us and, just like in domestic violence, we both turned on him." Tears began rolling down Old Peter's cheeks, but he ignored them.

"Those watches were the last presents your future selves exchanged ... I think they would have wanted you both to have them."

Peter and the two floating heads looked at each other somberly for a few moments.

"Now what?" Peter asked lamely.

"Now you two live your lives out happily ever after, like the brothers you are."

"What about you?" Cyril prodded.

"I don't know," Old Peter smiled gently. "This is all new to me. I'm just glad I think you two listened and will have a different outcome."

"You can stay here," Cyril offered. "You can be an older cousin or something."

Old Peter laughed. "Thanks, but I have meddled in your lives enough already. I was thinking more along the lines of a tropical island with a friendly indigenous population of beautiful women. Maybe a little fishing in the surf."

"Seriously?" Peter asked. "You can go anywhere, any when, and you are just going to go to the Bahamas?"

"The Bahamas? No. Close though! I was thinking more of Atlantis."

"Atlantis!" Peter and Cyril both laughed.

"Is it real?" Cyril asked.

"Oh yeah." Old peter nodded. "And you should see …"

Old Peter's voice faded out of Peter's attention as a woody smoke smell tickled his nose. Peter glanced out the door to the hallway just in time to see a yellow note hit the floor where only he could have seen it.

Peter's brow furrowed as he walked out into the hallway and into the last wisp of smoke. He picked up the note warily.

Don't let him do it!

Published Weekly.   NOW READY.   Price One Penny.

NOS. I AND 2 (TWENTY-FOUR PAGES), SPLENDIDLY ILLUSTRATED, IN HANDSOME WRAPPER.

The History of this Remarkable Being has been specially compiled, for this work only, by one of the Best Authors of the day, and our readers will find that he has undoubtedly succeeded in producing a Wonderful and Sensational Story, every page of which is replete with details of absorbing and thrilling interest.

On the Heels of Spring Heeled Jack

England
1877

"You sure this is a good idea?" Harland twisted at the corner of his handlebar moustache as he awaited Fitzhugh outside the water closet. He rested the palm of his other hand on the butt of the revolver on his right hip, an American fetish he wouldn't forgo.

"A marvelous idea! This is the best idea since the boar's hair toothbrush!" Fitzhugh stepped out of the water closet with a wide grin on his dark features. Englishman by birth and European by genetics, he was a man of the world by choice and delighted in the discovery of new things. "Harland! 'Tis amazing! Pull the lever and Presto! No more shite!"

"Not the kind from yer arse, anyways." Harland shook his head disgustedly. "You know that ain't what I meant."

"Yes, yes. No sense of humor—that is you, Harland." Fitzhugh glided past the American and back to the makeshift workshop housing the Time Destabilizer. He wore the clothes of a gentleman and took great pains to keep himself properly groomed. He had worked hard to instill the same sense of civility onto Harland. Stymied by the American's fashion choice of New England styles, Fitzhugh was nonetheless grateful for the improved hygiene.

"Right. And after two months you are still amazed with a new way to crap." Harland shook his head and turned back to the original object of discussion. "Look here. It's bad enough we destroyed the other workshop by means we can't explain the last time we traveled through time, but when I agreed to go back in time with you again, you

37

failed to mention we were going to use a damned Penny Dreadful as a map."

Harland held up a cheap publication. Its headline proclaimed 'Spring Heeled Jack: the Terror of London' and the illustration depicted several scenes of a devilish winged man pouncing out at hapless victims.

"Come, come, Harland. We both know the Time Destabilizer is working fine. We have tested many small jumps since then, and just because this publication is cheap entertainment for the masses doesn't mean the author isn't basing his facts on reality." Fitzhugh took the eight-page flyer from Harland as they entered the workroom and tossed it on a nearby workbench.

"I've seen the 'reality' what goes into those things, and there ain't none." Harland's mouth set in disgust.

"That is out in the Colonies! Things …"

"States." Harland corrected Fitzhugh.

Fitzhugh feigned to not notice and continued past the center of the room where the Time Destabilizer sat on a raised platform. Unimpressively shaped like a small hillock about three feet high at the center and ten feet in circumference, all of its internal mechanisms and distinguishing features were hidden under a wooden frame modified to hold various forms of camouflage.

"Things are different here in England. More civilized. People take pride in their integrity!" Fitzhugh brushed imaginary dirt from his suit as if making his point. He moved behind the wardrobe screen in the corner and began changing into his work clothing. "Speaking of which, please try not to insult Ursula again. I believe you have quite pushed her to her edge."

"Aw! Not that Kraut! I've still a belly full of her from the last time she—"

"There is that word again. Kraut. Why do you insist on being derogatory? And don't you feel foolish trying to insult her with food preferences?" Fitzhugh didn't wait for an answer, but instead crawled under the Time Destabilizer for final preparations.

Harland followed muttering "And I reckon being a Limey don't give you no never mind neither."

Not out of earshot as Harland had assumed, Fitzhugh responded with something unintelligible, but the word 'Yankee' was unmistakable.

As they worked together under the machine, Harland spent the next hour trying to talk Fitzhugh out of his plan to pursue Spring Heeled Jack, or at least to not involve Ursula. Eventually, a servant entered and informed them Lady Ursula had arrived.

"You're pokin' a hornets' nest," Harland pleaded one last time as Fitzhugh changed back into his suit to receive his guest. "She damn near cost us our lives last time, Fitzhugh. I think you should reconsider."

"That was a long time ago." Fitzhugh dismissed Harland's plea.

"Very funny. Yeah, that was a million years ago, as the time machine flies, but for me it was still last month."

Fitzhugh proceeded on to the parlor where Ursula waited, relishing in the attention of the servants as they opened and closed doors for them, met them with tea, and announced their arrival to Lady Ursula. Luxury was not new to Fitzhugh, but being the Lord of the Manor was something he was sure he would never get used to.

Harland did his best to ignore the servants and Fitzhugh's obvious pleasure at their presence. He knew it had been an unintended consequence of the accidental time shift that had occurred on their previous excursion into the past.

"Fitzie! Oh! It is so good to see you again!" Ursula's German accent had faded as she worked hard to fit into her new title of Lady. She even looked the part, resplendent in a frilly yellow summer dress. Harland wondered how she managed to move, yet she seemed to float as she moved to embrace Fitzhugh before giving Harland the barest of nods. "Harland."

"Ursula." Harland nodded back and did his best not to offend her as Fitzhugh had asked, so he said nothing else.

"I received your summons, *My Lord*," Ursula emphasized his title with a smirk, "and came at once! What would you have of me?"

"Lady Ursula," Fitzhugh made sure to use her new title so as to not upstage her entrance. "It is so good of you to come." He caught her elbow and began walking her out of the earshot of servants. Harland followed with a look of disgust on his face.

"As you are the only other person aware of the Time Destabilizer, you are singularly in a position to help us. We are about to embark upon a new adventure through time and, as you are already quite aware of the possible consequences, you would make the most suitable companion to accompany us."

Ursula stopped in her tracks. Her body posture changed completely, revealing she was, in truth, not a Lady. Cold stone eyes turned to Harland and her German accent shone through as all pretenses were forgotten. "Is he serious?"

Harland nodded and looked away.

"What the Hell is wrong with you, Fitz?" Ursula hissed at him. "Isn't this good enough for you?" She waved her hands around, encompassing the grand mansion. "What more do you want for God's sake? To be King? Even I got enough spoils from our last 'adventure' through time, and even if I hadn't, I'm not stupid enough to mess with it again!"

"Ursula, I told you before. I intend to use the Time Destabilizer for the good of mankind! For knowledge! Not for my own personal gain. That was never the intention and you know it." Fitzhugh managed to look offended yet appeasing at the same time. "If you do not wish to participate, you do not have to."

"Hmph!" Ursula eyed Harland. "That is what he has always said about the machine, but you! Look at you!" Her eyes rolled up and down Harland's clothes. "You look hardly different. Cleaner, a little perhaps, but still a grubby uncouth American. What are you getting out of this? Why did you build the machine?" She narrowed her eyes at him.

Harland pursed his lips and tried to remain civil. "I was in the wrong place at the wrong time," he drawled.

Ursula became irritated when he failed to elaborate. "It is plain to me you feel slighted you didn't profit the way we did," she indicated Fitzhugh and herself, "and that you plan to go back and change things more to your favor!"

Harland turned his head to spit in disgust before remembering the elaborate surroundings belonged to Fitzhugh. He cursed instead.

"Never mind," Fitzhugh interrupted Ursula's tirade. "We are perfectly capable of doing this without you. I merely had hopes you would have liked to join us on another adventure. Lady Ursula," he reminded her of her new title hoping it would cause her to reign herself in, "you are welcome to stay as my guest for as long as you wish. Harland and I will be off as soon our preparations are completed."

Fitzhugh gave her a bow and turned to leave. Harland followed. His relief she would not be coming had just started to set in when her voice carried after them. "You will not be cutting me out! I will be damned if I let you two go back and change things to cut me out!"

"This is much nicer than the stable we returned to before," Ursula stood in the center of the Time Destabilizer. Her face was dour, a consequence of losing the argument to wear her yellow dress. She now wore a commoner's drab functional dress appropriate to the time they were headed for. She was not thrilled to be back on top of the machine that had changed so much in her life.

"Hmmm. Not to mention it is not on fire. " Fitzhugh had changed clothes to match the style of a Gentleman forty years prior and was currently fussing with a piece of sod that wouldn't lie flat on the platform. Past experience had taught them to camouflage the Time Destabilizer platform as best they could and Fitzhugh was hoping to stabilize in a grassy area this time. "The damage to that building was extensive and makes no sense," he mumbled absently. "I am still planning how best to analyze what happened there. Are we ready, Harland?"

"You can never be ready enough to juggle cactus and rattlesnakes." Harland was underneath the Time Destabilizer platform making sure the connections were tight and everything was as it should be. He wore his old comfortable clothes, making him look and smell like most American cowboys of the last fifty years.

"If you don't know what caused all that damage, how can this contraption be safe?" Ursula's voice began to rise in panic.

"We have tested it several times for short little jumps to the middle of nowhere. It works fine." Fitzhugh assured her. "I suspect the damage was caused by the force of us arriving in an alternate timeline—one different than the one we left."

The machinations of the Time Destabilizer were beyond her comprehension. She had seen the underside, with its polished brass tubing and spinning contraptions, she knew what Fitzhugh and Harland had tried to tell her about using magnetism to melt crystals, and she had seen the unbelievable brilliant light leaking around the edges of the heart of the machine, but none of it made sense to her. It was beyond her imagination that Fitzhugh had found a way to make energy from magnets and water. She understood how to operate the machine and what she needed to get back home, and that was enough.

She made a conscious effort not to play with the pocket of her dress where she had placed the brass capsule necessary to bring the machine back to this time. It was too important to fiddle with.

"Well, now that you are ready to do more, why are we going looking for Spring Heeled Jack?" she asked Fitzhugh to keep herself from fidgeting. "Why not the Pharos, or the Greeks, or Romans? There are so many questions and things to be learned from them." Ursula's voice contained hints of facetiousness.

"I have always been fascinated by the legend. Was he real or imagined? A man or a beast? They claimed he could leap buildings and was impervious to bullets." Fitzhugh finished with the platform's camouflage and stood to join Ursula at the ready. "If he was a man, how did he do these things? I want to know!" Fitzhugh grinned at her. "Also, it is a fairly short trip through time, so we should be able to work out any problems that come up. I thought we should get our feet wet on something simple."

Harland joined them on the platform. Fitzhugh poked the tip of his cane down into the small open trapdoor that hid the controls, activated the machine, and knocked the lid shut with his foot. The Time Destabilizer began to hum with power. Fitzhugh adjusted his clothing one last time as he waited for the time distortion to wash over them. Ursula gave him a sour look.

"I still don't understand why I must dress below my station when you do not." Her tone was acidic but she had regained enough control to be using her new Lady-like English accent again.

"We all have a part to play, Lady Ursula, and we must dress for our parts." Fitzhugh planted his feet and used his cane to strike a steady pose of the perfect gentleman.

"What's my part?" Ursula asked as shimmers similar to heat waves began distorting their vision.

"Why, you are the bait, of course."

Harland smiled for the first time since learning Ursula would be accompanying them.

"Ach! It's cold! Where the hell are we?" Ursula demanded before Harland's vision had cleared.

Harland clenched his teeth and ignored her, keeping his hand on his gun while he assessed his new surroundings. They had appeared just inside the Barnes Cemetery and, except for being an out of place mound, the platform blended well with the tended grounds.

Fog swirled around them in the fading twilight making the cemetery gate seem ominous. The grey filled the night and quieted it, suppressing life and accenting the white of the headstones.

"We have not gone far," whispered Fitzhugh. "We are still in London. Nevertheless, I agree the chill of the approaching autumn is stronger than I had supposed. I hope we do not have to stay long."

Somewhere on the other side of the cemetery wall, lost in the mist, they could hear the sound of footsteps and walking cane on the cobblestones coming towards them.

"Where do we start looking?" Harland's hushed tones befit the setting.

"This is as close as I could pinpoint a time and location." Fitzhugh answered. "This was the first time anyone reported seeing Spring Heeled Jack."

A man's cry, not far away, broke the oppressiveness. "Good God!" The voice continued with a reflexive curse and then lamented through the fog. "I have laid eyes upon the Devil himself!"

Before Fitzhugh could direct Harland and Ursula to follow him and investigate, a maniacal giggling came from above their heads. They all looked up to see a dark shape coming out of the sky at them through the fog. Arms spread wide like batwings, it glided silent but for the laughter. Landing before them, it posed menacingly, obviously enjoying itself. An imposing figure of a man with a devilish appearance, including sprouting horns from its head and demonic wings under its arms, it was terrible to behold. A wicked grin split the pointed face. Chin, nose, and ears were sharp as daggers and its eyes glowed a horrible red. Then it froze.

"NO!" It cried out, holding up long clawed hands. "No! It cannot be! I killed you! I killed you all!" The voice was strange, distorted like a hissy buzz. The creature's posture changed as it prepared to attack.

Harland drew his gun but the creature was faster. Blue flame shot from its mouth in a bright ball, causing Harland to duck and his shot rang wild. A second ball of flame sent Harland rolling to dodge it. Before Harland could draw a bead on it again, the creature was upon him with a kick to the chest that sent Harland flying backwards into the darkness.

"Not this time, Harley!" the creature taunted and turned back to the others. "Useless as always, hey Fitz?" It circled dramatically with winged arms held high and wide as if ready to encompass them both.

"Who are you?" Fitzhugh demanded as he regained his composure.

"It's time to end it, Fitz. I've had enough of your games." The creature's glowing red eyes were eerie, reflecting off the fog and haloing its face wickedly. A strange reflection above one eye made Fitzhugh wonder if the face was a metal mask with a dent in it. Before he could get a good look the creature screamed again, "And most of all I have had enough of you! You conniving Bitch!"

It leapt at Ursula, swiping its razor claws at her as Fitzhugh leapt upon its back, grabbing a double handful of its cape. A great gash appeared across the pocket and pleats of Ursula's dress and the six-inch brass capsule fell to the grass.

Ursula gasped and fell as she grabbed her wounded thigh. Fitzhugh fell off the creature, tearing a sleeve open as he went, and landed hard on his back. As the creature scooped up the brass capsule from the ground, Fitzhugh saw the bare arm was nothing more than that of a man, and what was more, it had a half-healed bullet wound.

Harland stumbled back into sight with his gun swinging wildly looking for a target. The creature cackled again, flexed its knees, and gave a mighty leap in to the air disappearing into the murky night like a demon into the abyss.

"You are a fool to always let her carry the Boomerang, Fitz!" the creature laughed at them. "I can't believe she never left you behind, but I will! If I can't kill you, at least I can strand you here!"

Frustration tore at Harland's features. "What the hell was that?" he demanded.

Fitzhugh cradled Ursula's head in his lap. She was pale and frightened. She tried to rise up but found herself too weak to do so. "Is it bad?" she asked him hoarsely. "I cannot see it."

"I have not looked." Fitzhugh answered. "It would be impolite to raise a Lady's hem without first asking permission." He smiled gently at her.

"She screwed us again, Fitzhugh!" Harland's rage boiled as he confronted Ursula. "What the hell were you doing with the return canister?"

Anger flushed Ursula's face. Fitzhugh forestalled her comment by trying to lift her up. "Help us please, Harland."

"I got no help left in me for that teapot full o' piss." Harland spit to the side.

Fitzhugh met Harland's level gaze with one of compassion and hope. "I still have the return canister, Harland. Please help us. We can discuss this all later, in a safer place."

Harland held steady for a long moment then gave in and bent to help. He grunted once and fell to his knees holding his breath and his side.

"Harland? Are you injured?"

"Son of a bitch kicked like a fifty dollar mule." Harland grunted. He slowly stood up again then caught Ursula under the arm with one hand and pulled her to her feet.

Ursula's face was pale again as her eyes darted back and forth from Fitzhugh to Harland. "He knew us!" she hissed and clutched at Fitzhugh's arm. "He knew who we were!"

"I'm more concerned with what you were doing with our ticket home in *your* pocket and how he knew *you* had it there." Harland leaned threateningly in towards Ursula.

Ursula stuck out her chin and looked away.

"That was not the correct return canister." Fitzhugh reiterated and answered for her. "I still have the correct one right here in my pocket. As there was only one other canister, I have no doubts as to which was in your pocket, my dear Lady, but I am curious as to why."

The fog swirled about them as Ursula began to cry. "I was afraid you would go back and change things again!" she sobbed. "I thought you hated me and were going to leave me somewhere!" Her tears flowed and her words became incoherent. "I want to be a Lady! Don't make me not a Lady!"

Harland rolled his eyes and Fitzhugh hugged her tight and shushed her.

"Come on, Harland. Let us get back home and see if we can sort this out."

"So she had the return canister from our first trip?" Harland rubbed his eyes. Thinking about time travel made his head hurt almost as much as his ribs.

"Yes." Fitzhugh's answers were little help to Harland's headache.

"Because she thought we were going to take her somewhere and strand her there."

"Yes."

"And she thought she could use it to get back somehow if we left her behind."

"Yes."

Harland stared at Fitzhugh for a moment with his lips pursed trying not to be irritated. "So why shouldn't I just shoot her for almost getting us lost in time again?"

Fitzhugh lifted the damp cloth from Ursula's forehead and looked her in the eyes. She gazed back from the bed defiantly, thinking it was Harland lifting the cloth, but her eyes softened when she saw it was Fitzhugh.

"I believe that by having the return device in her pocket, she may have saved our lives." Fitzhugh smiled down at her. Ursula smiled and closed her eyes, pleased to let him defend her.

"How is this? Once again she steals our only way home, and once again you praise her for it! Damn it, Fitzhugh, we can't trust her!" Harland's voice rose so loud Fitzhugh stood up to meet him face to face.

"Harland," Fitzhugh spoke calmly, "we have a bigger problem right now."

"What shit in Satan's shorts could be more important?" Harland's mustache twitched in anger.

"Our deaths," Fitzhugh said coldly. "Didn't you hear that maniac claim he had killed us? I think he was genuinely surprised to see us. It is obvious he knew who we were. He knew what the return canister was *and* where to find it. There is no one outside of this room who could have known that. The only possible explanation is that we have just encountered someone from our future who wants us dead."

Harland, stunned, closed his mouth and took a step back. Ursula set up, all feigning forgotten.

"From our *future*?" Ursula asked.

"You said we can't go into the future!" Harland sputtered.

"Not with any accuracy, no, we cannot, but that does not stop someone from coming back from the future. We can go back to yesterday if we chose to, but tomorrow is inconceivable." Harland started to say something else but his eyes glazed as his thoughts raced.

"Why would we want to go back to yesterday?" Harland asked.

"You unimaginative slob," Ursula berated him. "We could bet on the horses or ..." she hesitated, "or we could go back and stop the fiend who attacked us! We could lay a trap for him!"

Harland shook his head. "You ain't learned squat from what happened to us last time we went back one day and ran into ourselves! You can't risk that! The only way to stop this is to never let it happen! We all hafta swear to never tell anyone else about any of this, then no one from the future will ever have the chance to come back and kill us."

"All right. Listen to me, both of you." Fitzhugh interrupted. "This is important. You are on the right track, Harland, we can't go back and interfere with ourselves, but you missed one important point. Someone has already come back to change things in their past and he thinks he killed us. He must have access to a Time Destabilizer or we couldn't have encountered him the way we did.

"As we have already found out the hard way, just because we can change the past and affect the things around us doesn't mean we have actually changed our own individual pasts. So, even if we change our own futures from here on out by destroying the machine, that maniac will still be out there with his own personal past—even if the future version of him is someone we never meet." Fitzhugh was on his feet pacing as he thought aloud. "So we must go back in time again and make him think he killed us. So if we go back to the second time anyone saw him and make him *think* he killed us, then he will realize that our last encounter took place *before* he killed us. Did you follow me?"

"No." Harland and Ursula answered in unison.

"We must confront this situation. There is no easy way around it." Fitzhugh stated flatly. "We must go back to the next time Spring Heeled Jack is recorded as having been seen and convince him of our deaths."

"How?" Harland asked the question on Ursula's mind.

A bright light flashed silently in the night before fading again. Fitzhugh's voice followed, ranging clearly through Clapham Common. "What the devil was all that light, Harland?"

The open space was empty of people. A creaking hackney continued away from them on the far side of the park, the hoof beats and wheels on the cobblestones echoing through the trees. The horse's twitching ear was the only indication anything had been noticed.

"Damned if I know!" Harland hissed. "It's your infernal contraption, you tell me!"

"I think you missed the Rookery stables by a bit." Ursula's voice was snide as she kicked at the hay covering the Time Destabilizer platform. It was obviously out of place on the groomed grounds and stood out in the dim glow coming from the distant gaslights.

"Be glad we didn't land in Long Pond!" Fitzhugh sounded uncharacteristically annoyed as he moved a hay bail and opened a panel near Ursula's feet. "Harland, fetch a light."

"Don't get your bowels knotted! I gotta fill the lantern. You said it warn't safe to travel with it full remember?" Harland hesitated a moment then cursed loudly.

Ursula squealed in rage. "You idiot! You spilt oil all over me!" She slapped at the oilskin in Harland's hand and it went flying, sending oil everywhere.

"Quiet down!" Fitzhugh hissed. "You two make enough noise to wake the dead!"

A dark figure swooped silently around them from tree to tree. "I never did believe what a debacle this night was for you until now!" The strange voice buzzed as red eyes glowed, disappeared, and lit again in new places as it gleefully cackled at them. I wish I could have seen the whole thing! Good bye, Ursula!" it laughed and shot a ball of blue flame from its mouth.

The blue flame hit Ursula in the skirts and she exploded into a screaming ball of orange flame.

Harland's first shot ricocheted off the creature's forehead in a shower of sparks, the second hit the arm, spinning the figure around before the creature leapt away at an astounding speed.

"You bastard, Harley! You shot me!" The voice came from behind and Harland twisted to see into the darkness just as the figure attacked heels first and sent him hurtling. The demonic shape righted itself, favoring one wounded arm.

"Fall down and roll!" cried Fitzhugh to Ursula. "Fall and roll!" He barely had time to see Ursula crumple to the ground when the sharp claws raked at him and spun him sideways.

He fell into the burning hay with crimson flowing all around him and a shocked look upon his face. Ursula flung herself around wildly screaming next to him, setting more of the hay ablaze.

Spring Heeled Jack stood for a moment and watched in fascination as Fitzhugh struggled to put out the flames on Ursula, instead spreading them to his own clothing. A shot rang out and the demonic figure lurched a step forward before catching its balance and leaping away, out of the reach of the firelight.

"Harland!" Fitzhugh called out. "Hurry! We are on fire! Help us!"

The flames streaked through the dried hay and caught on spilled oil sending them high into the night and blocking Fitzhugh and Ursula from view.

"I'm coming!" Harland limped towards the blaze. "I'm coming! Fitz!"

"No! Get away! The powder keg! Run away, Harland!" Fitzhugh cried desperately from inside the inferno. Ursula had stopped screaming.

"I'm coming, Fitz!" Harland dove into the flames with a defiant scream.

"No! No!" Fitzhugh cried.

The flame grew even higher as something else blazed. A blast wave sent burning straw high into the night and strange heat shimmers distorted the view. Then it was gone. Silence filled the night as a few straw embers winked out among the stars.

After a moment, a giggle broke the silence and a black shape appeared out of nowhere to do a dance on the empty spot where the bonfire had been. The laughter grew to a maniacal state before Spring Heeled Jack leapt away in an enormous bound. Laughing, he landed in front of the hackney coming up the road, sending the horse rearing in terror. The coachman, unable to keep control, was helpless as the carriage clipped a garden wall and overturned.

Spring Heeled Jack roared with delight as he leapt a nine-foot wall with ease and disappeared into the night.

Harland sputtered and choked on the water as he threw open the trapdoor. He grunted in pain and held his broken ribs. Fitzhugh sat up next to him. Soaked from the water tank hidden under the Time Destabilizer platform to extinguish their clothes, he got his bearings and worked to pull Ursula out.

Harland reached back to help and together they pulled her limp form out of the concealed hole.

"Is she all right?" Harland asked hoarsely.

Fitzhugh nodded. "I think she has just fainted. I did my best to hold her face into the air pocket."

They laid her down and stripped the ruined dress from her thin form. Fitzhugh had to stop and remove his shredded leather vest he had filled with cochineal dye and honey as the tatters hampered his movements. The vest Ursula wore had cracked with the heat and the honey had crystallized, but the asbestos suit underneath was intact, giving Fitzhugh a strong sense of relief.

Harland stripped his own vest off and began removing his own asbestos suit. "Do you think it worked?" he winced in pain as he struggled with the shirt.

"We are alive, are we not?" Fitzhugh responded while removing his own protection.

"Mostly," Harland glanced down at Ursula's limp form. "She did a good job. I'm sorry it was her he chose to set on fire, but she played it well."

"Why Harley, I do believe that is the first kind thing you have ever said about me." Ursula blinked up innocently at Harland.

"Don't call me that."

Ursula sat up and put a hand to her head. "Ach! My head hurts! I told you this hood was too tight!"

"It is likely oxygen deprivation. It should soon pass." Fitzhugh commented absently. "Harland? I thought we agreed you wouldn't shoot him unless you had to."

"I had him dead to rights. I know I hit him at least twice."

"Yes, but what if you had caused another time ripple, killing him before he had met us at the cemetery?" Fitzhugh admonished him.

Harland snorted. "What's one more little time ripple, *Lord* Fitzhugh?"

Fitzhugh started to answer then stopped, his mind racing. "Time ripple," he muttered.

"What?" Harland had seen that look before, and it wasn't good.

"He was coming back in time. The bullet wound on his arm! You just shot him but it was half-healed the first time we saw him! He can't interfere directly with his own past, so if he fails, he has try somewhere else. He was moving further back in time ... but we saw him for the last time the first time we saw him ... so we had to have already seen him!"

"What are you babbling about?" Ursula sat up.

Fitzhugh stood up and ran out of the workshop. Confused, Harland and Ursula hurried to follow as he raced out of the manor and towards the stables. They found him digging furiously at the pile of scorched wooden beams that had once been the original workshop.

"Fitz! What are you doing?" Ursula tried to calm him but he shook her off and kept pulling debris from the mess.

"He would not have stopped! When he discovered we had not been stranded, he would have tried again! Even further back in time, in our past!"

"What are you carrying on about?" Harland demanded.

"Oh my God." Fitzhugh stumbled and fell back, dropping the burnt beam he had been moving. "He did."

"He did what?" Ursula stepped forward and then gasped.

Harland looked down into the rubble pit Fitzhugh had exposed. A tangle of half-charred corpses lie crushed under the debris, still gruesomely recognizable. "That's us," he muttered. "That sonofabitch killed us."

"Not us." Fitzhugh hung his head. "Those people belonged in this timeline. That is the real Lord Fitzhugh and Lady Ursula. We filled the void they left behind ..."

"So ... Is he still after us?" Ursula asked quietly, her breath quick and shallow as she tried not to faint.

Fitzhugh stared at the bodies despondently. "Only time will tell."

Support Independent Artists

Things are different now. Things are changing, and we need your help. Independent artist's books won't be found in a bookstore or a supermarket. It's all we can do to get on Amazon or Barnes and Noble. Please, rate us, review us, tell others about us. Go to Amazon, B&N, Goodreads, Kobo, Smashwords, or anywhere else you like to look for books, and tell us, and everyone else, what you thought about our books. Please be honest. Review the book, don't bash the author or make irrelevant statements. Don't accept pirated copies. Don't buy pirated copies. Why give money to the thief and put an author you like out of business? Most authors make very little money and work as a labor of love (truth be told, most authors never turn a profit). Tell your friends about the books you like. Support the authors you want to see more from. Blog about them. Tweet and Facebook about them. Ask your library and local bookstore to carry their books. In the age of the internet, the reader —YOU— have the power to make or break an author. Really. One person could do it. Use it. Use that power well, and use it responsibly.

If you read one of my books, and you review/rate it, let me know, and I will send you a short story to thank you. Just be honest with your review. You can reach me at sam@samknight.com. Thank you for your support.

—Sam Knight

Why I Write

This post originally appeared on <u>The Fictorians</u> *blog on May 4, 2013. This is a question I get asked often, especially after people find out how much money most writers DON'T make. Most of us never break even on the costs of putting ourselves out there, and even the better known authors make only a moderate income. Yeah, I know, J.K. Rowling, Stephen King ... Those are people who won the lottery. Actually winning the lottery is easier. According to sources I won't admit to quoting because I don't trust the internet, there are 1600 $1 million or more lottery winners every year. How many big name authors can you name?*

The next time you read a 'review' of a book that is nothing but slander against the author, please remember to take that into account before you allow someone else to pass judgment for you.

My grandfather and my mother are avid readers, so I came by that honestly. Writing however is a different story.

I have a tendency to get sick. I mean really sick. If everyone else in the house has a sniffle, I have a cold. If they have colds, I have the flu. If everyone has the flu, I'm at the doctor's. The problem with getting that sick, that often, is you get bored really stinking fast.

Being a child in the 70's, I didn't have video games until Pong came out, and I could play that for only so long. Television was only worth watching for about two hours a day, and then only on some days (except Saturday morning cartoons!). Books though ... they worked 24/7.

One particular illness sticks out in my memory. I was in fifth grade and down sick with what I was told was the 'Russian Flu.' I was miserable sick—except when I was reading. When I was reading, I was in another world. I could literally forget about my own problems! I would be so engrossed, the rest of the world ceased to exist. That was a godsend.

That was also my first real introduction to the idea of a 'series' where the story continued on into the next book. The world didn't come to an end when I closed the book, there was another one waiting!

I read Patricia A. McKillip's Riddle Master Trilogy, Piers Anthony's Xanth Trilogy (back when there were only three), a trilogy collection of Edgar Rice Burroughs' John Carter books, and three or four of Alan Dean Foster's Pip and Flinx series. When I ran out of new books, I re-read The Hobbit.

It was quite an eclectic mix, and I read them all in a little over a week. And then I went looking for more. Everything I could get my hands on. Up until that time, I had been a 'reader'. I had read the Hobbit and The Lord of the Rings in Fourth grade. But now, after doing so much reading, so intensively, I had become addicted. I had become a biblioholic. I had to have more!

I raided my mother's bookshelves and then I headed for my grandfather's. I came away with armloads of Andre Norton, Robert Heinlein, Kenneth Robeson, Frank Herbert, and more.

Some sucked me in, other's not so much. I was searching for authors with a specific talent—the ability to make me forget I was reading a book. I was actually trying to recreate what I had experienced while I was ill.

Yeah, I read the things the other kids were reading. The Mouse and the Motorcycle, Charlie and the Chocolate Factory, and the like. They were good, but … they didn't transport me into another world the way I wanted.

I wasn't in the game to read about little problems with kid brothers, or mysteries about missing toys. I wanted the Hero's Journey. I wanted books that let me see Star Wars in my head. (We couldn't just buy it and watch it anytime we wanted back then. Not to mention that, if I remember right, Star Wars was around $100 when it came out on VHS five or six years after theatrical release, and a brand new book was only $3.50.) I wanted books that let me live a different life.

And I found them. I found a lot of them. I started with authors I already knew could make a movie behind my eyes, and I got everything I could by them. I read Piers Anthony's older sci-fi stories, and then I followed all of his new series as they came out. I followed Alan Dean Foster's Pip and Flinx adventures all the way until 2009 when he finally wrapped it up. I'm still waiting for David Gerrold to finish The War Against the Chtorr series (not holding my breath though…) Along the way, I found Robert Asprin's Myth series, Lawrence Watt-Evan's Ethshar books, Terry Pratchett's Discworld, and more.

I worked 60 hours a week while attending college full time, and I still made time to read. I would exchange books with co-workers. I gave away my copy of Douglas Adams' Hitchhiker's Guide to the Galaxy just to convince someone to read it, and then I went and bought myself another. I did that three times.

After I graduated, I carried my book du jour to work with me and read it during my lunch hour. At first my new co-workers laughed at me, but by the time I left there were close to a dozen people doing the same thing.

Why? Because books are magic. A well-crafted book made by a talented author will cast a spell over a reader and transport them to a new place, a different time, another life.

That's what I was looking for when I was sick. A different life. And those wonderful authors gave it to me, even if it was just for stolen moments at a time. They gave it to me. And as I lay in that bed so many years ago, a thought drifted through my mind. A thought that stayed with me the rest of my life.

I wanted to return the favor. I wanted to write something that could bring as much joy to those authors as they were giving me.

Ideas began bouncing around in my head after that. When I worked physical labor, I would entertain myself by thinking up stories. When I drove long distance, I would stay awake by imagining new places, new worlds, and new people. Eventually, I found that nearly anything would give me a story idea.

And soon, very soon, I will finally move beyond my apprenticeship and craft a story that repays my heroes. I will inspire the next generation, and honor the previous. I will write because I read, and it was wonderful.

Author Biography

Photo by Stacey Vowell

A Colorado native, Sam Knight spent ten years in California's wine country before returning to the Rockies. When asked if he misses California he gets a wistful look in his eyes and replies he misses the green mountains in the winter, but he is glad to be back home.

His grandfather and mother are avid readers and Sam says his own passion started when he pressed his grandfather to find out what was so interesting. His grandfather handed him a book and he has been an avid reader ever since. He claims to have finished the Hobbit and the Lord of the Rings trilogy in fourth grade and says he can still remember the look, feel, and smell of some of those early books. (He has been spotted sniffing books as he ruffles the pages.)

While doing research for a Western novel, Sam was not surprised to find out that, once upon a time, half of his family had been on the wrong side of the law. It stands to reason that when your great-great-grandfather was a marshal in Cripple Creek, Colorado, someone in the family had to be a horse thief. Sam was, however, surprised to find the family name had originally been McKnight and that the thieves had taken the 'Mc' part of the name with them. (Or the lawmen let them have it to distance themselves from that side of the family.) Having served a stint working in a correctional facility, he has often wondered if being a lawman runs in the blood. His great grandfather upheld the law in Mooreland, OK, as well as Springfield and Florence CO, among other places, with his grandfather occasionally deputized to assist.

When asked why he would want to become a writer, Sam recounts a time when he was in fifth grade. Illness stuck him in bed for two weeks with only books for companions. (This was a bit before video game phone implants were in common use.) He burned through the Xanth trilogy (back before it expanded into thirty some books), the Riddle of Stars trilogy, a couple of John Carter of Mars books, and several Pip and Flinx novels, relishing the moments when he would become so engrossed he would forget the ills of the physical. A thought floated through his mind at that time, about being able to return the favor to the authors who were providing so much to him. That thought never left and now he sincerely hopes anyone picking up one his stories can find something they were looking for.

Drop in and see what he is up to at SamKnight.com. If you have something you want to say, leave a comment, or contact him at sam@samknight.com

Author Bibliography

Published by Knight Writing Press:
Four Adventure!
Time Travel Trio

Stories in anthologies available now:
The Maltese Dragon
Captain Samjack's Terror Emporium

Stories a little bit harder to find:
The Copper Colored Hummingbird
The Cat Lady and the Dragon
A Small Town Santa

Things that are *Free*:
Broken (A Flash Fiction Piece)
Boutonnière (A Flash Fiction Piece)
Steam Punk Nursery Rhymes

Coming Soon:
A Whiskey Jack in a Murder of Crows
Lucid Nightmares Part 1: Bedeviled

Links to find or purchase can be found on the author's website:

SamKnight.com

Are You Still Reading This Stuff?

A reward for your dedication!

A free short story can be found on my website at: samknight.com/?page_id=1270.

The name of the story is Catching the Dead Eye Special.

I entered the NYC Midnight 2013 Short Story Challenge, going up against more than 800 other writers. (I didn't win.) For this competition, I was assigned to write a story, 2,500 words or less, within the following guidelines: Genre: Horror, Subject: a flight on a private jet, Character: a drug dealer. I had less than a week to do it. Some have suggested that I needed to turn this into a much longer story to do it justice. Come visit my website, read the story, and let me know what you think in the comments section.

www.ingramcontent.com/pod-product-compliance
Lightning Source LLC
Chambersburg PA
CBHW071210130626
46555CB00004B/1657